For all at Holy Family School,

Southampton

M.C.

For Carrie Rose

G.W.

JP

LITTLE TIGER PRESS
An imprint of Magi Publications
1 The Coda Centre, 189 Munster Road, London SW6 6AW
First published in Great Britain 1998
This edition published 1998

Text copyright © Michael Coleman 1998
Illustrations copyright © Gwyneth Williamson 1998

Michael Coleman and Gwyneth Williamson
have asserted their rights to be identified as the author
and illustrator of this work under the Copyright,
Designs and Patents Act, 1998.

Printed in China

ISBN 978-1-85430-950-1

3 5 7 9 10 8 6 4 2

One, Two, Three, Oops!

by Michael Coleman
illustrated by Gwyneth Williamson

LITTLE TIGER PRESS
London

Mr and Mrs Rabbit had a big family . . .

A *very* big family . . .

A very, *very* big family!

"I wonder how many babies we've got?"
said Mr Rabbit one morning. "I think I'll
count them."

"Why not wait until later?" said Mrs Rabbit.

"I would."

"No," said Mr Rabbit firmly. "I'll do it now."

So outside he went to where the babies were
playing. Mr Rabbit started counting.
"One, two, three – oops! Oh, noggin-sploggin!"
he exclaimed.

With a hop and a skip, the babies he'd counted ran off to join their brothers and sisters. He couldn't tell which ones he'd counted and which he hadn't.

Mr Rabbit started again. This time he got
a little further. "One, two, three, four – oops!
Oh, noggin-sploggin, boodle-doodle!" he
grumbled.

The babies had started a game of tag
and moved. He'd lost count again.

Mr Rabbit tried one more time.
"One, two, three, four, five – oops!
Oh, noggin-sploggin, boodle-doodle,
grizzly-wizzly!" he groaned.

The babies had started playing hide and seek.
Now he couldn't see any of them. He'd lost
count again.

"This is no good," said Mr Rabbit. "I'll have
to think of a better way."

So he sat and thought – until he had a good idea.
"I know," he said. "I'll give a carrot to every baby
I count. That way I'll see the ones I've missed."
So Mr Rabbit started counting again. This time he
gave a carrot to each baby he counted. "One, two,
three, four, five, six – oops! Oh, noggin-sploggin,
boodle-doodle, grizzly-wizzly, sniffy-whiffy!" he cried.

The babies he'd
given carrots to
had eaten them!
He couldn't tell
who he'd counted
and who he hadn't.

"I know," said Mr Rabbit,
as he had another good idea.
"I'll tell them to sit down
when I've counted them.
That way I won't get
mixed up."

So Mr Rabbit told his babies to sit down once he'd counted them. "One, two, three, four, five, six, seven – oops! Oh, noggin-sploggin, boodle-doodle, grizzly-wizzly, sniffy-whiffy, jingle-bingle!" he shouted.

The ground was full of prickly weeds.
Just as soon as a baby sat down, it jumped up
again! Mr Rabbit had lost count once more!
"Right, this will *definitely* work," said Mr Rabbit,
as he had yet another idea. "I'll send every baby
indoors. The ones still outside will be the ones
I haven't counted. I can't possibly get muddled
up that way!"

So Mr Rabbit started counting again. This time, every baby he counted was sent indoors.
"One, two, three, four, five, six, seven, eight – oops! Oh, noggin-sploggin, boodle-doodle, grizzly-wizzly, sniffy-whiffy, jingle-bingle, fuddle-duddle!" yelled Mr Rabbit, stamping his foot.

He'd forgotten that their home had
a back door. Every baby he'd sent in
the front had run straight out the back.
He'd lost count yet again.

Mr Rabbit sat down and thought once more. He thought all afternoon . . .

. . . and he thought all evening. And then he noticed a patch of mud on the ground and had his best idea yet.

"I've got it!" said Mr Rabbit. "Every time
I count a baby I'll put mud on its tail.
Then I'll know that the babies with clean
tails are the ones I haven't counted. I can't
possibly get muddled that way."
So Mr Rabbit began to count once more.
Every time he counted a baby, he put a
blob of mud on its tail. "One, two, three,
four, five, six, seven, eight, nine – oops!
Oh, noggin-sploggin, boodle-doodle,
grizzly-wizzly, sniffy-whiffy, jingle-bingle,
fuddle-duddle, jungle-bungle!"
he roared, jumping up
and down . . .

It had started to rain. All the blobs of mud he'd put on the babies he'd counted had been washed off. He'd lost count yet again!

"I give up!" said Mr Rabbit. He stomped angrily back indoors. "I don't know *how* to count those babies!" he cried. "I'm fed up!"

At that moment Mr and Mrs Rabbit's babies
scampered back indoors. Tired and happy after
playing all day they were soon fast asleep.
"I told you to wait till later," said Mrs Rabbit.
"Now try counting them."

Mr Rabbit began counting once again.
"One, two, three, four, five, six, seven,
eight, nine, TEN!" he cried. "I've done it!"
"Oh no you haven't," said Mrs Rabbit . . .

"You've forgotten the littlest ones!"

Reading is fun With Little Tiger Press

THE LONG
JOURNEY HOME
David Bedford and Penny Ives

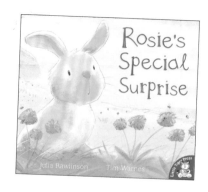

Rosie's
Special
Surprise

Julia Rawlinson   Tim Warnes

SLEEP TIGHT,
GINGER KITTEN
Adéle Geras
Catherine Walters

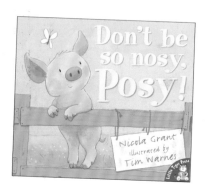

Don't be
so nosy,
Posy!
Nicola Grant
illustrated by
Tim Warnes

Sleepy Sam
Michael Catchpool
illustrated by
Eleanor Taylor

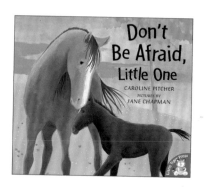

Don't
Be Afraid,
Little One
CAROLINE PITCHER
PICTURES BY
JANE CHAPMAN

Tim Warnes
George
&
Sylvia

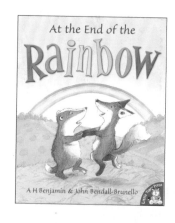

At the End of the
Rainbow
A H Benjamin & John Bendall-Brunello

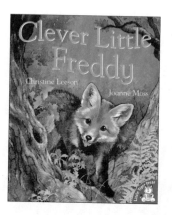

Clever Little
Freddy
Christine Leeson
Joanne Moss

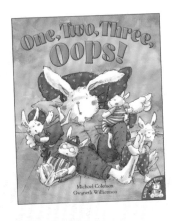

One, Two, Three,
Oops!
Michael Coleman
Gwyneth Williamson

for information regarding any of the above titles
or for our catalogue, please contact us:
Little Tiger Press, 1 The Coda Centre,
189 Munster Road, London SW6 6AW
Tel: 020 7385 6333 fax: 020 7385 7333
E-mail: info@littletiger.co.uk www.littletigerpress.com